Contents

	A Note About This Story	4
	The People in This Story	6
1	The Storm	7
2	The Pilot	10
3	Darryl's Idea	14
4	Facts and Memories	18
5	'What Do You Want Me To Do?'	22
6	The Museum	26
7	The Phantom Airman	31
8	The Message	35
9	'Glen Did This'	39
10	The Battle in the Sky	44
11	The Diary	49
12	The Ops Room	52
13	Gone for Ever!	57
14	The Kids	59
	Points for Understanding	62

A Note About This Story

The four friends in this story go to the same school. They are all members of their school's archeology club. Archeology is the study of how people lived many years ago. Archeologists dig in the ground. They try to find the things which people used and the places where they lived.

The friends are going to write a project for their club. The project is going to be about their town in the Second World War (1939 to 1945). During this time, Britain and Germany were enemies. The armies, navies and air forces of Britain and Germany fought each other. The British air force was called the Royal Air Force (RAF). The German air force was called the Luftwaffe. Some RAF pilots flew 'Spitfire' fighter planes and some Luftwaffe pilots had 'Messerschmitt 109' fighter planes. There were many battles between fighter planes in the air above northern Europe. The worst was the Battle of Britain in 1940. It lasted from June to October. Many hundreds of people died.

Fighter planes were quite small. But there were larger planes – bombers – which carried big bombs. These bombs were dropped on towns and cities. Some of the German bombers were called 'Dorniers'. Some of the British bombers were called 'Lancasters'.

Pilots in the RAF worked together in groups – squadrons. The pilots flew their planes from small airfields. Each airfield had a few concrete runways and some large buildings for the planes. Many other people worked in buildings on or under the ground of airfields. People in a tall building called a control tower gave instructions to the pilots and they watched the planes. In Operations Rooms (Ops Rooms), men from the RAF and women from the WAAF (Women's Auxiliary Air Force) worked. On large maps, they marked the places where planes were at all times. They gave this information to the officers in charge of the fighting.

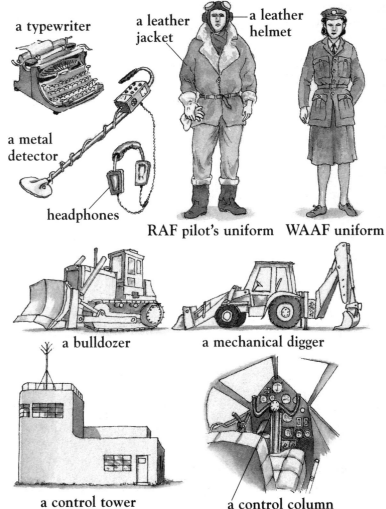

a typewriter

a leather jacket

a leather helmet

a metal detector

headphones

RAF pilot's uniform

WAAF uniform

a bulldozer

a mechanical digger

a control tower

a control column

The People in This Story

Frankie Fitzgerald   Jack Christmas   Tom Christmas

Regan Vanderlinden   Darryl Pepper

Jennie St Clair   Mrs Fitzgerald   Florrie Skinner

George Ballard   Terry Bowles   Mrs Bowles

Glen Loosthawk   Squadron Leader Alfred
Leighbridge-Smith

1

The Storm

Four young people – two girls and two boys – were standing in the long grass in the middle of Lychford Green airfield. The airfield wasn't used any more and all its buildings were in ruins. Their roofs had fallen and their walls were broken. Grass and weeds grew in broken places in the concrete runways. The airfield's gates were shut. They hadn't been opened for many years. But the wire fence around the airfield was broken in many places. The kids had walked through one of the broken places.

It was raining, and the kids were cold and wet.

'This doesn't *look* very exciting,' one of the girls said. 'But it will be a good subject for our project.'

The girl who had spoken was Frankie Fitzgerald. Frankie – a pretty, fair-haired girl – was thirteen years old. The other girl was eleven-year-old Regan Vanderlinden. Her hair was dark. The two boys, Jack and Tom Christmas, were brothers. Jack was thirteen and Tom was twelve. Both were fair-haired.

'This is a very sad place!' Jack Christmas said. 'Something terrible happened here once. Perhaps it happened during the Second World War.'

Jack often said things like this. He often knew things which he couldn't explain. Sometimes he knew what was going to happen *before* it happened. Sometimes he knew what had happened in the past, without being told about it.

'Take your photos quickly, Tom,' Jack said to his brother. 'Then we can all go home. I don't like it here.'

7

Tom Christmas looked around carefully. Then he lifted his camera and began to take pictures.

Suddenly, the younger girl ran in front of Tom.

'Hi! Take a picture of *me*!' she shouted.

'Get out of the way, Regan,' Tom replied. 'I want to take photos for our project. I don't want pictures of a crazy American kid.'

Regan's blue eyes were shining. She laughed and pushed her long black hair away from her face.

'There's plenty of time for the project,' she said.

'No, there isn't. We've only got two weeks,' Tom said. 'Today is the 24th of August. We have to finish the project by the 6th of September. And we haven't *started* it yet.'

The four friends went to the same school. They were all members of the school's archeology club. Their history teacher, Mrs Tinker, was in charge of the club. She'd asked all the members of the club to do a project during the summer holiday. They all had to find out about the history of their town of Lychford between the years 1939 and 1945. That was the time of the Second World War.

Frankie Fitzgerald had told her three friends about the airfield. Lychford Green airfield, which was at the edge of the town, had been a very important place during the War. Frankie knew about it because she had lived in Lychford all her life.

So Frankie, Jack, Tom and Regan had decided to do a project about the airfield together.

'My grandmother was a young girl during the Second World War,' Frankie said, as they looked around the wet, ruined airfield. 'Gran remembers the Battle of Britain, in 1940. Spitfire fighter planes flew from this airfield to fight

8

the Luftwaffe – the German air force. The airfield was a busy place then.'

'It's just a ruin now,' Regan said.

'We'll see the airfield better from above,' Frankie went on. 'Darryl is trying to arrange a plane flight for us. He has a friend who flies an old plane.'

'That will be brilliant!' Tom said. 'I'll be able to take more photos from the plane.'

The rain was falling heavily now and a strong wind was blowing. Suddenly, there was a flash of lightning. The sound of thunder followed it at once. The four friends were in the middle of a terrible storm.

'Run!' Tom shouted. 'Run back to Darryl's van!'

As the kids ran towards the fence, lightning turned everything white again. Then there was a tremendous noise. They were all thrown to the ground.

Regan looked up and screamed. A black shape was falling out of the dark clouds. Tom looked up too.

'It's a Spitfire!' he shouted. 'And it's going to crash!'

Another flash of lightning showed the Spitfire more clearly. Flames and smoke were coming from the engine of the falling plane.

'No! No!' Regan shouted.

At that moment, the plane hit the ground.

2

The Pilot

Regan jumped up and ran. But she didn't run towards Darryl's van, she ran towards the other side of the airfield. There was only one thought in her mind – the pilot. There was a pilot in that plane. And the plane was on fire – it was burning. They had to get the pilot out!

Soon, Regan was near enough to see the plane clearly. The Spitfire had crashed about two hundred metres outside the airfield. It had crashed onto a small house.

Regan screamed when she saw this, but she ran on. Then she saw a black shape on the grass, about twenty metres in front of her. The shape moved and stood up. It was a man. He was wearing a leather jacket and a leather helmet. It was the pilot!

The shape moved and stood up. It was the pilot!

Regan screamed again. The pilot looked at her, then he ran towards the house. He tried to get into the house, but the flames from the burning plane were too hot.

'Help me!' the man shouted. 'The children are in there!'

Regan saw a flash and heard a terrible roar. Flames jumped high into the sky. The pilot was lifted into the air for a moment. Then he crashed onto the ground. The house was on fire now, but the plane had gone.

Regan ran to the pilot. The airman's clothes were burnt and torn. Regan saw his face. It was terribly cut and burnt. But his eyes were open. The pilot was still alive.

'We must get Darryl and the van here now!' Regan shouted to her friends, who were running towards her. 'We must take this man to a hospital.'

The four friends ran back across the airfield. The storm was almost finished. The sky was getting lighter. Now, they could see their friend Darryl Pepper, sitting in his old van by the airfield gates.

'What's wrong?' Darryl asked.

'Didn't you hear anything?' Regan asked. 'A plane crashed onto a house on the other side of the airfield. The pilot is badly injured. We must take him to a hospital.'

The kids jumped into the van and Darryl drove it through a broken place in the fence. Soon they were on the other side of the airfield.

'Which way shall I go now, Regan?' Darryl shouted. 'I can't see a house anywhere. Where is it?'

Regan opened her mouth but she couldn't speak. There was no house, no plane, no pilot – there was nothing.

Darryl stopped the van. Suddenly, the sun was shining. A bird began to sing. The four kids and their friend got out of the van.

'What exactly *did* you see?' Darryl asked.

'It began with the storm,' Jack said.

'What storm?' said Darryl. 'There wasn't a storm.'

'What about the thunder? What about the lightning? What about the rain?' Jack replied.

'There was a little rain,' Darryl said. 'But there was no thunder or lightning.'

'And what about the plane crash?' Regan said. 'We all saw it and heard it. Were we all dreaming? Did we all have the same dream?'

'The plane was a Spitfire,' Tom said. He knew a lot about old planes.

'And it crashed near here, onto a house just outside the fence,' Regan went on. 'The pilot had got out of the plane but he ran back towards the house. He spoke to me. He said something about some children. He spoke with an American accent.'

While Regan and Tom had been talking to Darryl, Jack had walked through a broken place in the fence. Suddenly he shouted to the others.

'Come over here!' he said. 'Look at this. There was a house here once, a long time ago. You can see the shape of its walls on the ground. It's a ruin now and it's covered with grass and weeds. But there's terrible sadness here. Something terrible *did* happen here once.'

Regan turned away. 'I don't want to stay here any more,' she said.

Silently, they all got into the van. Darryl drove very carefully back into Lychford.

'*Did* we all have the same dream?' Jack asked.

'No, it wasn't a dream,' Regan said. 'We *didn't* all see

13

the same things.' In her mind, the American girl could still see the cuts and burns on the airman's face.

3

Darryl's Idea

Darryl Pepper lived in a big room at the top of an old house. Darryl was the kids' friend. He was nineteen years old, but some of his hair was already grey. He had a long, thin body and long, thin legs. He wore thick glasses.

Darryl had been a student at the kids' school. He'd been the first member of the archeology club. He was very interested in history and science and he had many books about these subjects. He didn't work in an office or a factory. But he often delivered things for people in his old van. He earned some money that way.

Darryl's room was full of old furniture, books, papers and pieces of machinery. His computer stood on a big desk near a window. The rest of the desk was covered with papers.

———

Regan, Frankie, Jack and Tom met in Darryl's room on the morning after their visit to the airfield.

'Well, who can explain what happened yesterday?' Jack asked.

'I have an idea,' Darryl said. 'Some scientists have a theory which could explain it. It's the Psychic Stain Theory.'

'What's that?' Tom asked quickly.

Darryl's room was full of old furniture, books, papers and pieces of machinery.

'Well, sometimes a terrible thing happens and it leaves a mark in time,' Darryl replied. 'The mark never disappears. It's like a stain that never fades. Then the terrible thing is repeated for ever and ever. The theory could be correct. Lots of people believe in ghosts. Perhaps ghosts are Psychic Stains too.'

'So that crash *did* happen. But it didn't happen yesterday. Is that what you think, Darryl?' Jack asked.

'Yes,' Darryl replied. 'It happened in the past and it left a mark in time. Now it's like a videotape which is playing again and again. And yesterday, you all saw it.'

'But why hasn't anyone seen the crash before?' Frankie asked. 'I've lived in Lychford all my life. I've never heard anything about it.'

'That's an interesting question,' Darryl replied.

'I want to find out more about that crash,' Regan said. 'When did it happen? Who was the American pilot?'

'I've been asking some of my friends about this,' Darryl said. 'There *are* a few Spitfires still flying. They fly in air shows and exhibitions. But no Spitfire has crashed in this area since 1945. So your Spitfire probably crashed during the Second World War.'

'Perhaps it was in a battle with a German fighter plane,' Tom said.

'That poor pilot,' Regan said. 'He tried to save some children who were in that house. Were they all killed?'

Jack remembered his feelings about the house.

'Yes, they were all killed,' he replied sadly.

'I want to know what happened,' Regan said. 'Where can we find out about this, Darryl?'

'Well, that crash was "repeated" yesterday for a good reason,' Darryl said. 'Why? What was the reason?'

16

'Was the date important?' Tom asked. 'Yesterday was the 24th of August. Did the crash happen on the same date, many years ago?'

'Yes, that's exactly what I think,' Darryl replied.

'Then we can make some guesses,' Tom said. 'The first Spitfires flew in 1938. The Second World War began a year later, in 1939. The War ended in 1945. So the crash happened sometime between 1938 and 1945.' Then Tom looked puzzled. 'But Spitfires were British planes,' he went on. 'Why was an American pilot flying the one that we saw?'

'My grandmother might remember something about the crash,' Frankie said. 'I'll ask her about it. I'm going to visit her this afternoon.'

'I've got a better idea,' Tom said quickly. 'Let's ask someone at the Lychford newspaper – the *Lychford Gazette*. Jack and I will go to the office of the *Gazette*. We need facts, not just memories. Does the *Gazette* office keep copies of the old newspapers, Darryl?'

'Yes,' Darryl replied. 'I have a friend who works there. I'll phone him. He'll let you look at the papers.'

'And I'll go with Frankie, to see her gran,' Regan said. 'I prefer old people to old newspapers!'

'That's fine,' Darryl said. 'Then, you'll have the facts *and* the memories.'

'Brilliant!' all the children said together.

'Let's meet tomorrow at my house,' Regan said. 'Will four o'clock be OK?'

4

Facts and Memories

'Hello, Frankie dear. What a nice surprise!' old Mrs Fitzgerald said. 'And you've brought Regan with you. Sit down, both of you. We'll all have some tea.'

In a few minutes, they were all drinking tea and eating biscuits. Frankie began to speak about the project.

'We went to the old airfield yesterday, Gran,' she said. 'We're doing a project about the Second World War for our archeology club. We're trying to find out about the fighter planes that flew from Lychford Green. We're trying to find out about the pilots too. What do *you* remember about the War, Gran?'

'I remember lots of things,' the old lady replied. 'The airfield was very busy then. There were lots of planes there. The pilots were all tall and good-looking. They came into my mother's shop sometimes.'

'Do you remember a plane crashing near the airfield?' Frankie asked.

'Oh, yes,' the old lady replied. 'The pilot died and so did some evacuees. My mother told me about it. It was very sad.'

'What were evacuees?' Regan asked.

'During the War, the Germans often bombed our cities,' Mrs Fitzgerald said. 'So lots of children from the cities were sent to live in the countryside. They were called evacuees. Their parents wanted them to be safe from the bombs. London was bombed almost every day. Lots of children from London were sent to this area. The four children who were killed came from London. They were sent to Lychford to be safe.'

Regan and Frankie looked at each other. So it was all true! The plane *had* crashed onto the house by the airfield. Five people *had* died, nearly sixty years ago. But the four friends had seen it happen yesterday!

'Why did the crash happen, Gran?' Frankie asked.

'I don't know,' Mrs Fitzgerald replied. 'I was only five years old in 1940. But Florrie Skinner will remember. She's much older than me. But she remembers everything from those days. Florrie was a WAAF during the War.'

'A what?' Regan asked, with a laugh.

'She was in the Women's Auxiliary Air Force,' the old lady said. 'The members of that were called WAAFs. WAAFs didn't fly the planes, but they did important work. Florrie worked in the Operations Room on the airfield. That was the place where the movements of all the planes were organized.'

'Where does she live, Gran? Can we talk to her?' Frankie asked.

'She lives in an old people's home,' Mrs Fitzgerald replied. 'She lives there with lots of other old people. She's not strong now, and the nurses at the home look after her. But she enjoys having visitors. I'll take you to see her tomorrow morning. We can't go now. It's after two o'clock, and Florrie always sleeps in the afternoons.'

—————

Half an hour later, Frankie, Regan, Jack and Tom were in the Vanderlindens' sitting-room. Regan had given each of her friends a can of cola and a bag of potato crisps.

Regan's parents were very rich. They owned a big house in Lychford. But most of the time, Mr Vanderlinden worked in other countries. This summer, he was working in Rome and his wife was there with him. Regan was living in the big house in Lychford with an eighteen-year-old blonde girl from California.

The girl was the Vanderlindens' *au pair*. She was called Jennie St Clair. Her job was to look after Regan. But Jennie wasn't clever and she didn't work hard. She made a lot of expensive phone calls to her boyfriend in the USA, but she didn't care about Regan. So Regan looked after herself, and she had a great time! But Regan didn't like Jennie. When she talked to her friends about the *au pair*, she called her by a rude name – the Blonde Bimbo!

When they had finished their crisps, the girls told the boys about Frankie's gran and about Florrie Skinner.

'We're going to visit Florrie tomorrow,' Regan said. 'What did you find out at the newspaper office?'

'Well, the crash happened on the 24th of August, 1940,' Jack said. 'And your gran was right. The Spitfire crashed onto a little house near the airfield. Four young evacuees from London were killed.'

'The pilot died too,' Tom told the girls. 'And he *wasn't* an American. He was a Canadian. His name was Glen Loosthawk.'

'Why was he in England in 1940?' Regan asked.

'He was studying at a university here when the war started,' Jack said. 'Glen joined the Royal Air Force. He was only twenty years old when his plane crashed.'

'He was very unlucky,' Tom went on. 'He'd been in a battle with some German planes. His radio wasn't working and suddenly there was a terrible storm. He crashed onto the house. A lot of fuel was stored there. The fuel exploded and everyone was killed.'

'The crash wasn't the pilot's fault,' Regan said quickly.

'Well, Glen Loosthawk made a mistake – that's what the newspaper said,' Tom replied. 'It was only Glen's third flight in a Spitfire.'

'It *wasn't* Glen's fault,' Regan said again. 'And he tried to save those evacuees. I saw him running towards the house.'

'The newspaper didn't say that,' Tom said.

'No, it didn't,' Regan said. '*We're* the only people who saw the crash. And we only saw it *two days ago*!'

'Those evacuees were the same ages as us,' Jack said. 'They were thirteen, twelve and eleven. There were two boys and two girls. The boys were brothers, like Tom and me.'

'That's terrible!' Frankie said. 'They left their parents in London. They came to Lychford to be safe, but they were killed here. Poor kids!'

'And poor Glen,' Regan said. 'No one else will ever know the truth about him now. He was a good man. Perhaps Florrie Skinner knew him. We'll ask her tomorrow.'

'We've still got a lot to do,' Tom said. 'Darryl is trying to borrow a metal detector for us. If we search the airfield with that, we'll find all kinds of things. There must be pieces of planes in the ground. Anything that we find can be part of our project.'

'Perhaps Darryl will arrange that flight for us too,' Frankie said.

'Yes. That will be great,' Jack replied. 'Tom and I will put all our notes onto our computer tomorrow. You two girls can talk to the old lady at the old people's home.'

5

'What Do You Want Me To Do?'

Regan was asleep in her bed. She was dreaming. In her dream, she heard the roaring engines of planes and the thud of exploding bombs. The ground was shaking. She smelt smoke and she saw flames. She heard screams and the sounds of people running.

'Stop! Stop! Come back! Don't leave me!' she shouted. Then a dark shape was standing in front of the flames. It was a man. It was the dead pilot – Glen Loosthawk! In her dream, Regan looked at his terrible, burnt face and she screamed.

Suddenly, she was awake.

But the ground was still shaking. Regan got out of bed. She walked towards the window and pulled back the curtains. There was a red glow in the dark sky. The glow was over Lychford Green airfield.

Regan turned away from the window. She got dressed quickly and went downstairs. Ten minutes later, she was on her bike, cycling to the airfield. The night was fine and clear.

The American girl reached the airfield, and left her bike by the gates. She found a broken place in the fence and walked through it. Almost immediately, heavy rain started to fall. Then Regan heard a voice.

'Help me! For God's sake, help me! The children! The children!'

The voice was coming to her from across the airfield.

Regan closed her eyes for half a minute. Then she opened them again. Nothing had changed.

'I'm *not* asleep,' she said to herself.

'The children!' the voice shouted again. Regan started to run across the airfield. After a moment, she saw the burning house.

'I can't help you! It's too late!' she shouted.

Lightning flashed. Thunder roared. The heavy rain fell on her face. But she went on running towards the flames.

Then the pilot was standing in front of her. There was blood on his face. His clothes were burnt and torn.

'What do you want me to do?' Regan shouted.

The man took a step towards her.

Regan screamed. Then she turned and ran back towards the gates. But suddenly the pilot was standing in front of her again. Regan tried to turn, but she slipped

23

and fell to the ground. A hand touched her shoulder.

Regan looked up. 'What do you want me to do?' she said again. This time she spoke quietly.

The man pointed towards the burning house.

'I can't do anything,' she said. 'It's too late. It happened nearly sixty years ago.'

Regan stood up and started walking. Soon she was near the fence. As she walked through the broken place in the fence, the rain stopped. The night was fine and clear again. But Regan was wet and very cold. She got on her bike and rode slowly home. She was shaking with cold and fear.

'I must tell the others about this,' she said to herself. 'But they must finish the project without me.'

—

'So that's why I'm not going to the airfield again,' Regan said. 'I had to see you and tell you.'

It was the next morning. The four friends were in Jack and Tom's house. Jack, Tom and Frankie had heard Regan's story.

'The pilot was trying to tell you something,' Tom said. 'Why did you run away from him?'

'I was terrified!' Regan replied. 'I was very, very frightened. I'm not going back to the airfield.'

'OK,' Tom said with a smile. 'If you're afraid, you don't have to help us.'

'I *want* to help you,' Regan replied angrily. Then she was silent for a few moments. When she spoke again, her voice was quiet. 'I will go back to the airfield, if you all come with me,' she said.

'OK!' said Tom.

Then the phone rang and Jack answered it. When he put the phone down, he smiled at the others.

'That was Darryl,' he said. 'He's arranged our flight. His friend will take us up in the old plane tomorrow.'

'Brilliant!' Tom said.

'Darryl told me something else,' his brother went on. 'There's a private museum at the Lychford Country Club. It tells the story of Lychford Green airfield during the Second World War. Darryl has arranged for us to go there. We can go now.'

'*You* two go there,' Regan said. 'Frankie and I will talk to Florrie Skinner. We'll all meet at my house later.'

6

The Museum

Jack and Tom were standing in the little museum at the Lychford Country Club. Outside, members of the club were playing tennis and swimming in the pool.

An old gentleman with a big white moustache was smiling at the boys.

'My name is George Ballard,' he said. 'I worked at the airfield during the war. I was a Flight Sergeant in the Royal Air Force. Please look around the museum. Ask me questions if you want to.'

'Thanks,' Tom said. 'Look at these pictures, Jack!' He pointed to some photos which were hanging on a wall. 'This is a Spitfire fighter plane. And this one is a Lancaster bomber.'

'You're quite right,' George Ballard said. 'Now look at this —'

———

The old man was happy to talk to the boys. He wanted to show them everything in the museum. Jack wrote notes and Tom asked a lot of questions.

At the far end of the room, George Ballard stopped in front of a big photo of the airfield. The photo had been taken from the air.

'This picture was given to us by some friends in Germany,' George Ballard said. 'It was taken by a German airman in a Dornier bomber, just after the Luftwaffe attacked the airfield on the 28th of August, 1940. Look, you can see the three runways very clearly.'

'What are all those white marks?' Tom asked.

'Those are bomb craters – the big holes made by the German bombs,' George Ballard replied. 'The Operations Room – we called it the Ops Room – was hit by a big bomb too. A lot of people died on the 28th of August. The Station Commander died too. His name was Squadron Leader Alfred Leighbridge-Smith. This is a photograph of him.' George Ballard pointed to a smaller picture. It showed a middle-aged man wearing RAF uniform.

'So the Squadron Leader was in charge of the airfield when the Spitfire crashed onto the house by the fence,' Tom said.

George Ballard looked very surprised.

'How do you know about that?' he asked.

'We found out about it for our school project,' Jack said quickly.

'It was sad,' George Ballard said. 'The pilot made a mistake. He was a young man and he'd only flown a Spitfire a few times. And the weather was terrible too. He was unlucky.'

Jack moved on. He looked down into a cabinet with a glass top. Inside it, there were more photos, an old watch, a leather flying helmet and then – an empty space! In the space was a small card with the words:

NOTEBOOK BORROWED BY MR TERRY BOWLES

Jack put his hand on the glass. It was very, very cold. Suddenly he knew something. The notebook that had been in the cabinet was very important.

'What was here, Mr Ballard?' he asked.

'Squadron Leader Leighbridge-Smith's diary,' George Ballard replied. 'The Squadron Leader's grandson, Mr Terry Bowles, has borrowed it. He's a businessman. He's a very clever man too. The diary was written in a secret code. And Terry Bowles has discovered the secret of the code. He's going to write a book about his grandfather. The diary will help him with that. But he hasn't told anyone what's in the diary yet.'

_____

Regan and Frankie were at the old people's home, talking to Florrie Skinner. The old lady was blind – she could no longer see anything. But her mind was clear. She was very happy to talk to the girls. She remembered many things about the War. She remembered the Luftwaffe's attack on the airfield on the 28th of August, 1940.

'I was working in the Ops Room when the bomb hit it,' Florrie said. 'I was lucky, but some of my friends were killed. That was a terrible day. I had bad dreams about it for years afterwards.'

'You must have some very sad memories,' Regan said.

The old lady smiled. 'Yes. But they aren't *all* sad,' she replied. 'I had a lovely boyfriend. He was a Canadian and he was very good-looking. I'll never forget him.'

'A Canadian,' Regan said. 'What was his name?'

'Was his name – Glen Loosthawk?' Frankie asked quietly.

Florrie Skinner smiled again. 'Glen,' she said. 'Yes, that's right, Glen. I've got a photo of him. Would you like to see it?'

'Oh, yes, please,' the two girls said together.

The old lady walked slowly across the room. She sat down on her bed. Her fingers found an old red box on the small table beside it. She opened the box and took out a big envelope.

'Here are my photos,' she said. 'Come here and sit on the bed. Find the picture of Glen.'

Frankie opened the envelope and looked through the old photos. The first ones showed Florrie as a little girl. Then there was one which showed her as a pretty young woman in WAAF uniform. And next, there was a photo of a young airman. He was tall and very good-looking. Frankie turned the picture over. On the back were the words: *GLEN – 21ST JULY, 1940.*

Regan took the photograph and looked at it. The American girl's eyes were full of tears.

'Have you found the picture of Glen?' Florrie Skinner asked.

'Yes, we've found it,' Regan said quietly.

'That was the last picture that I took of him,' Florrie said. 'He was killed soon afterwards. And four children died the same day. They were evacuees. They were lovely children. Glen and I had become good friends with them. They died on the same day as Glen, but I saw them in the Ops Room, four days later. That was the day of the German attack.'

'You saw the evacuees *after* they were dead?' Frankie said.

'Yes. They were wearing strange clothes, but I knew them,' Florrie replied. 'They looked like living children, but they were ghosts. Poor little ghosts!'

The Phantom Airman

The four friends met again in the afternoon. They had a lot to talk about.

'That diary sounds interesting,' Frankie said. 'I'd like to see it.'

'We could phone Mr Bowles,' Jack said.

Regan had been very quiet. She suddenly stood up and began to speak.

'I've got to go to the airfield,' she said. 'I've got to find out what Glen wants.'

'When will you go?' Jack asked.

'Not at night,' she replied. 'I'm too scared to go at night. I'm going *now*.'

'Then we'll all go with you,' Frankie said.

'Well, thanks,' Regan said. 'But please remember this. Glen's face is frightening. You haven't seen it, I have.'

'Don't worry,' Jack said. 'We'll all do this together.'

'Come on,' Frankie said. 'We'll all go on our bikes.'

But when they got to the airfield, everything there had changed. They got off their bikes by the old airfield gates.

'What's happening?' Tom asked.

There was a big sign on the gates.

FACELIFT CONSTRUCTION

is building Lychford Green Industrial Estate here.
We're building a new future for Lychford.

PRIVATE - KEEP OUT

Some of the fence had gone. There were trucks and a big bulldozer standing by the ruins of the control tower. There were some mechanical diggers and a big roll of new fence wire. But there were no workmen anywhere.

'What about our archeology project?' Frankie said. 'We won't be able to get onto the airfield when these people start work.'

'And what about Glen?' Regan asked. 'I've got to speak to him again. I'm going to do it now.'

Regan started to walk across the airfield.

'Come on!' she called to the others. 'This is our last chance!'

Frankie, Jack and Tom followed her.

'That little hill on the right is where the Ops Room was,' Tom said. 'We found out about it at the museum. The RAF built the Ops Room and some offices under the ground. Then they covered the roof with earth. They tried to make it safe. But the bomb hit it on the 28th of August, 1940, and several people were killed. We can't get in now. The entrance was covered with earth years ago.'

Regan went on walking for a moment. Then she stopped and shouted into the air.

'Glen! I'm here. I want to help you.'

There was silence. The four friends waited. Suddenly, a shape appeared in front of them.

'Look!' Regan whispered. 'It's Glen.'

Regan began to run towards the ghost.

Glen was wearing his leather jacket and helmet. But this time, his leather helmet covered his face.

'He's done that to help me,' Regan said to herself. 'He doesn't want to frighten me.'

The phantom airman pointed across the airfield.

'Yes, that's where it happened,' Regan said. 'What do you want me to do?'

The ghost began to fade away.

'Glen! Don't disappear!' Regan shouted. 'Please don't go, Glen! What do you want? You must tell me!'

But the phantom airman had gone.

'He wants you to look over there,' Jack said. 'He was pointing to the ruins of the old house.'

Regan walked on towards the ruins, looking down at the grass. She felt a hand on her shoulder and she turned quickly. But there was no one there.

'Glen?' she said quietly.

Regan pushed at the earth with her foot. She could see a piece of metal in the ground. She bent down and pulled the piece of twisted metal from the earth. The metal was very, very cold.

'Did you want me to find this, Glen?' she asked.

'Hey! You over there!' a man's voice shouted. Regan turned quickly. A fat man was walking towards her. He wasn't a ghost! Jack, Frankie and Tom walked over to Regan. The four friends stood close together.

'What are you doing here?' the fat man shouted. 'This land is private!'

The man was about forty. He had a round, red face and he looked very angry.

'Can't you children read the sign?' the fat man shouted. 'What do they teach you at school these days?'

'They teach us to find out about things. They teach us to think,' Regan said, with a smile. 'We are working on an important archeology project about the Second World War. We haven't finished studying this airfield yet.'

'Oh, yes, you have,' the man said angrily. 'This land belongs to Facelift Construction now.'

The man took a mobile phone out of his pocket.

'Are you going to leave, or shall I call the police?' he asked.

Regan opened her mouth, but Jack spoke quickly.

'Please don't do that,' he said. 'We're leaving now.'

The four friends walked slowly back to their bikes. The man stood and watched them.

8

The Message

The kids went back to Regan's house.

Regan put the piece of twisted metal on a table in the sitting-room. They all looked at it in silence for a few minutes.

'Come on, do something,' Regan said to the piece of metal. Nothing happened.

'Do you want it to talk to you?' Tom asked.

'I want it to help us,' Regan replied.

Ten minutes later, the piece of metal hadn't done anything.

'Oh, come on!' Reagan said. 'Let's go into the kitchen and get a drink.'

Soon, they were all sitting round the kitchen table with cans of cola.

'We're going up in the old plane tomorrow,' Tom said. 'I'm glad about that. If I can't take any more photos *on* the airfield, I'll take some from the air *above* it.'

'We won't be able to use the metal detector, though,' Frankie said sadly.

'Oh, let's just forget about the project,' Regan said angrily. She got up suddenly and went back into the sitting-room. A moment later, the others heard her screaming.

'Come here! Come here quickly!' Regan shouted. 'It's moved! The metal has moved!'

Frankie, Jack and Tom ran into the sitting-room. They all stared down at the table. One word had been scratched into the shiny wood: TRAITOR.

'Was there a traitor at the airfield?' Jack said. 'Was someone there helping the Germans? Is that what Glen is telling us.'

'Let's go back into the kitchen,' Tom said. 'The message probably isn't finished yet. Perhaps the metal will write some more, if we don't watch it.'

'It might write some more, but not on this table!' Regan replied. 'My parents paid more than two thousand dollars for it in New York City. I'm taking the metal upstairs, to my bedroom.'

She picked up the piece of metal carefully and the others followed her upstairs. Regan put the piece of metal on a desk near the window in her room.

'We'll leave it alone now,' she said. 'We'll go back to the kitchen and I'll cook some pizza.'

During the next two hours, Regan went up to her bedroom several times. The metal hadn't moved.

At last, it was evening. Jack and Tom had to go home. But Frankie decided to stay at Regan's house for the night. She phoned her mother with this news.

Late in the evening, Jennie St Clair came home. She had been out of the house for most of the day. Now she went straight to her own room.

'The Blonde Bimbo will be watching TV all night,' Regan said. 'She doesn't care what I do. Why does my father pay her?'

After that, the two friends went up to Regan's bedroom again. The piece of metal still hadn't moved.

There were two beds in the room, and each girl sat on one. Later, they heard Jennie go downstairs. Soon the house was quiet again.

Then the piece of metal began to move! It moved slowly over the top of the desk – *scratch, scratch, scratch*. The girls watched it from their beds. They couldn't speak – they were terrified.

Suddenly, the bedroom door was opened wide.

'You stupid, stupid kid!' Jennie St Clair shouted. 'You're crazy, that's what you are. You've wrecked that table in the sitting-room. It must have cost your parents thousands of dollars. I'm going to phone your mother about this – now!'

The piece of metal had stopped moving at the moment when Jennie came into the room. Regan was glad about that. She didn't want the *au pair* to see it.

'It was an accident, Jennie,' Regan said. 'Someone can repair the table. I'll pay for the work myself.' Suddenly her voice was angry. 'Don't phone my mother, Jennie,' she said. 'If you do, I'll tell her a few things about *you*. You watch TV all the time and phone people in the US. You don't look after me at all. I'll tell my mother *that!*'

Jennie was very angry. She went towards Regan's bed, but then she saw the scratches on the desk.

'You're wrecking the furniture in here too!' she shouted. She ran to the desk and picked up the piece of metal. Then she turned and left the room with it. She closed the door behind her with a loud noise.

'Come back here! Give me that!' Regan shouted. She opened the door and ran downstairs after Jennie.

Frankie got up and walked over to the desk. She wanted to see what the piece of metal had written now.

She saw a line of letters, scratched into the wood.
HELPMERESTSAFEUNDERTHEAIR

'Help – me – rest – safe – under – the – air,' Frankie read.

'What does that mean? I don't understand,' she said to herself.

She heard the front door close with a loud noise. Regan was coming back upstairs. A moment later, she came into the bedroom.

'Do you know what Jennie has done?' Regan shouted. 'She ran out of the house. Then she threw that piece of metal into a truck that was passing. Can you believe that? The metal has gone for ever. How can we help Glen now?'

'Well, the metal did write several words,' said Frankie. 'They might help us. Come and see.'

Regan looked at the letters on the top of the desk.

'I don't understand,' she said. 'I'm tired. Let's go to bed now. We'll phone the boys about this in the morning.'

9

'Glen Did This'

Back at their house, Jack and Tom were talking about Glen's strange message – TRAITOR. What was the phantom airman trying to tell them?

'Perhaps there was a traitor on the airfield,' Tom said. 'I want to see the Squadron Leader's diary. We might learn about the traitor from that.'

'Yes,' Jack replied. 'But there's something strange about the diary. I'm sure of that.'

'Let's phone the Squadron Leader's grandson, Terry Bowles. Give me the phone book, Jack,' his brother said.

Tom read out the number and Jack dialled it. In a few moments, a woman's voice answered. Jack asked for Mr Bowles.

'I'm sorry, Mr Bowles isn't here at the moment,' the woman said. 'I'm his wife. Can I help you?'

'I'm not sure,' Jack said. 'My name is Jack Christmas. My friends and I are doing a project about Lychford airfield in the Second World War. There was a traitor on the airfield in 1940. Someone in the RAF was working for the Germans. But we don't know who it was. We'd like to see Squadron Leader Leighbridge-Smith's diary. Can we speak to your husband about it when he comes home?'

Mrs Bowles laughed.

'There was no traitor,' she said. 'I've been helping my husband with his work on the diary. There's nothing in it about a traitor. You've watched too many spy films, Jack! But tell me your phone number. I'll ask my husband to phone you, when he has time. He's very busy at the moment.'

Jack put down the phone.

'We won't get any help from Mr or Mrs Bowles,' he said. 'Let's finish putting our notes onto the computer. We'll talk to the girls about this in the morning.'

———

In the middle of the night, Regan woke up suddenly. Something strange was happening. She was falling through the air and her room was full of smoke.

She fell to the ground, but she wasn't hurt. She had

fallen very gently. But now, part of her bedroom was on fire. She saw flames moving through the room.

The flames moved nearer and nearer to the terrified girl. And then they covered her.

Now Frankie was awake too. She heard noises – guns firing, and loud explosions that shook the room. Huge flames were everywhere. They were on the walls, on the curtains and all round her bed. And Regan had gone! Where was she?

Frankie opened her mouth, she was going to scream. Then she saw Regan. The American girl was walking through the flames towards her.

'The flames are cold,' Regan whispered, as she sat on Frankie's bed.

Then the bed started to move. And all the other furniture in the room started to move too. It turned round and round. Everything was covered in flames. But the flames were as cold as ice!

Suddenly there was silence. No noise. No flames. The two girls sat on the bed and looked at each other. The room was wrecked. Everything was on the floor – books, clothes, magazines.

Regan pushed her long black hair away from her face.

'Hi!' she said.

'What happened?' Frankie gasped.

'Glen did this,' Regan replied. 'He's angry because we didn't get all of his message. Perhaps —'

She didn't finish her sentence because they heard a terrible scream outside the door.

'Jennie!' Reagan shouted. She ran to the door and pulled it open.

Outside the bedroom, Regan and Frankie saw Jennie.

She was floating above their heads. She was turning round and round in a strong wind. And as they watched, the wind pushed Jennie to the top of the stairs.

'No, Glen! No!' Regan shouted. 'Don't hurt her!'

The wind stopped and Jennie fell gently to the floor. She stared at the two friends for a moment. Then, without speaking, she got up and walked into her own room. She shut the door behind her.

Regan and Frankie went back into Regan's room. Together, they put everything in its place. Nothing had been broken. Nothing had been burnt.

Then the two girls lay on their beds and fell asleep immediately.

———

Frankie and Regan were still asleep when the boys rang the doorbell the next morning. When the girls were dressed, everybody went into the kitchen. Regan told Jack and Tom what had happened.

'Why did you let Jennie throw away the piece of metal?' Tom asked Regan. 'Now we've only got half a message. And we can't understand it.'

At that moment, the kitchen door opened and Jennie came into the room.

'Hi, Jennie,' Regan said. 'You look terrible.'

This was true. Jennie looked tired and frightened.

'You must tell me something,' Jennie said. 'In the middle of the night, did I wake up on the floor outside my room? That's what I remember. You were there. I saw you. But perhaps I was dreaming. I *was* dreaming, wasn't I, Regan? It *was* all a dream?'

'Yes,' Regan replied. 'You were dreaming.'

'Thanks,' Jennie said. 'I'm going back to bed now.'

When Jenny had gone, Regan laughed. 'We won't have any more trouble from the Blonde Bimbo,' she said. 'Now, what are we going to do about Glen?' She repeated the message again. 'It says, "Help me rest safe under the air—" Perhaps the next letters were going to be f-i-e-l-d. Is Glen buried under the airfield? Does he want us to stop the construction work?'

'No, Glen can't be buried *there*,' Jack said. 'Perhaps Glen was going to write two sentences. Perhaps he wanted to say, "Help me rest safe. Under the airfield—" But he didn't tell us what was under the airfield.'

'There must be *something* under the airfield,' Tom said.

'And Glen wants us to find it,' said Frankie went on. 'Perhaps it's something about the traitor.'

'We *must* go to the airfield again,' Jack told the others. 'I want to use that metal detector there.'

'Perhaps Darryl will have some more ideas,' Regan said.

'We'll ask him,' Jack replied. 'We're meeting him at one o'clock. We're going up in the old plane this afternoon. Tom has brought his camera.'

10

The Battle in the Sky

The kids were in Darryl's van. They were on their way to the airfield at Halleyford, about thirty kilometres from Lychford. Darryl was very interested in Glen's message.

'I agree with Tom and Frankie,' he said. 'There is something important under Lychford Green airfield. Glen wants you to find it.'

Suddenly, there was a loud noise in the sky above

them. For a moment, a dark shape covered the sun.

'It's a Spitfire!' Tom said.

'It's Glen!' Regan whispered.

Darryl laughed and shook his head.

'No, it isn't Glen,' he said. 'That's a real Spitfire. It flies from Halleyford airfield. We're nearly there now.'

'It's a real plane? Good,' Jack said. 'The past and the present are getting very mixed up!'

Darryl and the kids were going to fly in an old plane – a De Havilland Dragon Rapide. There were eight seats for passengers in the plane, but they were very close together. Darryl and the kids climbed in. The heaviest people sat at the back, the lightest in the front. The pilot got in last. Regan was sitting nearest to him.

The pilot started the engines and the old plane began to move. And then they were in the air.

The children looked down. The cars on the roads were tiny. The little fields were green, yellow and brown squares.

'We'll soon be over Lychford Green airfield,' Darryl shouted after ten minutes. The noise of the engines was loud and he had to shout. 'Get your camera ready, Tom.'

The pilot took the plane lower. Now they could all see the airfield. They could see the old control tower and the other broken buildings. They could see the little round hill above the underground Ops Room. There were the three runways. And *there* were the Facelift Construction trucks. But there were no people working on the airfield.

'Facelift Construction hasn't started work yet,' Jack said to himself. 'Perhaps we *will* be able to use the metal detector. We really must get onto the airfield again.'

'Have you taken your photos, Tom?' the pilot shouted.

'Yes, thanks. I've used all the film,' Tom said.

'OK. I'm turning back now. We don't ...'

———

Suddenly, there was complete silence. Had the plane's engines stopped? Frankie turned round quickly. Jack was shouting at her. She could see his mouth moving, but she couldn't hear his words. Behind Jack, Darryl was sitting very still. His eyes were open, but he wasn't seeing anything.

Regan and Tom were shouting now, but Frankie couldn't hear them either. Jack pointed at the pilot. Regan touched the man on the arm. The pilot didn't move, but the plane flew on. What was happening?

There was a dark shape in the sky, coming towards them. Then there were *two* dark shapes. And close behind them were two more. They were planes.

Tom knew what the planes were. They were Messerschmitt 109s – German fighter planes from the Second World War! The Messerschmitts had guns and now they were shooting at the Dragon Rapide. The kids saw the bullets hitting the wings of the plane. But there was still no sound.

'Is this happening now or in the past?' Jack asked himself.

The Dragon Rapide turned slowly. Now it was going down. The ground was coming nearer and nearer.

Frankie quickly unfastened her seat belt. She moved carefully towards the pilot. He was holding the control column in his hands, but he was not controlling the plane. Frankie put her hands over his hands, and tried to pull the column back. It was very difficult, but at last the control column moved. Soon, the plane was flying

The Messerchmitts had guns and now they were shooting at the Dragon Rapide.

straight ahead again.

And now there were three more planes in the sky. They were Spitfires! The first Spitfire fired its guns. Its bullets hit one of the German planes and the Messerschmitt began to fall.

———

Then suddenly, the sky was empty. The Dragon Rapide's engines were roaring loudly. The children could hear the wind again. And the pilot was speaking.

'... have much fuel,' the pilot was saying. 'Have you all enjoyed the flight? Was it exciting?'

'Oh, yes, we enjoyed it very much,' Frankie replied. 'It was *very* exciting.' And the kids all laughed.

———

When they were back in Darryl's van, the four friends told him what had happened.

'Was that battle another Psychic Stain?' Jack asked him.

'No. Glen made that happen,' Darryl said. 'He was probably telling you to do something. But what?'

'If Glen can do that, he must be very powerful,' Regan said. 'He can take us into the past whenever he wants to.'

'Perhaps *we* are giving Glen his power,' Jack said.

'Yes, that's possible,' Darryl replied. 'Well, I'm going to get that metal detector for you this evening. Where do you want to go now?'

'Take us to Radnor Road, please,' Jack said. 'I want to visit Mr Terry Bowles.'

'Why?' Regan asked.

'I want to see that diary,' Jack replied. 'The diary is very important. I'm sure about that!'

11

The Diary

Radnor Road was in a new part of Lychford. The Bowles' house was a large, modern one. There was a high fence around the house and garden.

The four friends walked up to the front door. Jack rang the doorbell twice, but there was no answer.

He turned away from the door and began to walk to the back of the house. He had to get inside. The others followed him.

At the back of the house, there was some white furniture in the garden. And there were two tall glass doors, which led into the house. They were not locked. Jack pulled open one door and took a step into a large room.

'Wait for me here,' he said to the others.

The room was an office. Jack could see a desk, a computer, a metal cupboard and lots of bookshelves.

There was a strange, frightening feeling in the room. For a moment, Jack wanted to leave. Then he saw a small green notebook on the desk.

'That's the Squadron Leader's diary,' Jack said to himself. 'I must read it.'

He walked slowly towards the desk. It was very difficult for him to move now. Something wicked was trying to stop him.

Jack's fingers touched the diary. It was very, very cold ...

Suddenly, it was night – dark, dark night. At first, Jack couldn't see anything. Then he knew where he was. He was standing in the middle of Lychford Green airfield. He was near the control tower. But it wasn't a ruin, covered with grass and weeds. It was a *new* control tower. There were other new buildings nearby. Jack heard a car passing a few metres away. Then he heard people walking about. He was back in 1940!

Two hundred metres away, Jack saw some large shapes. They were black against the dark sky. He had seen the ruins of these buildings from the air, earlier that day. Aircraft were kept in them, he knew that. He walked towards them.

When he was near the first building, Jack heard a sharp noise inside it. He went quietly into the building. There were several Spitfires inside.

Jack stood under the wing of the nearest Spitfire. A man was working on the plane. Immediately, Jack knew something about him. He was a wicked man!

Jack waited. After a while, the man finished his work and he turned around. Jack could see the man's face now. The boy had seen that face before – in an old photo at the museum. It was the face of Squadron Leader Leighbridge-Smith. The Squadron Leader was the traitor at Lychford Green airfield!

'This Spitfire is Glen Loosthawk's plane,' Jack thought. 'Today is the 23rd of August, 1940. On the 24th, Glen's plane will crash. He will die and so will the four evacuees. The Squadron Leader broke something inside Glen's plane. He is a murderer!'

———

'... and what are you doing in my house?' a woman's voice was shouting. 'How did you get in here?'

Frankie, Tom and Regan were in the room with Jack now. The woman who was shouting at them was wearing a bathrobe. A towel was tied around her head.

'We rang the front doorbell,' Tom said quickly. 'There was no answer, so we came round to the back of the house.'

'You walked into my house while I was taking a bath!' the woman shouted. 'I'm going to call the police.'

'No, please don't do that,' Jack said. 'My name is Jack Christmas. I phoned you yesterday. I wanted to talk to your husband.'

'My husband is busy at the airfield,' Mrs Bowles said. 'He isn't going to speak to you.'

'He's at the airfield?' Regan said. 'Does he work for Facelift Construction?'

'My husband *owns* Facelift Construction,' Mrs Bowles replied. 'Now get out of my house – all of you!'

There was nothing more that the children could do.

They walked slowly down Radnor Road. As they were walking along, Jack told them his story.

'So the Squadron Leader was the traitor,' Regan said. 'Mr Bowles must know about it. He knows what's in his grandfather's diary. He understands the code. That's why he doesn't want *us* to see the diary.'

'But why did the Squadron Leader kill Glen?' Frankie asked.

'Glen found out the truth,' Tom said. 'So the traitor killed him. It's simple.'

'And the proof of the traitor's wickedness is under the ground somewhere on the airfield,' Regan said quickly. 'Mr Bowles knows that, and he is looking for the proof too. But we must find it first!'

12

The Ops Room

It was 5.30 the next morning. The sky was getting light. Darryl had driven the kids up to the airfield gates. The gates were shut and locked. And there was a new wire fence all around the airfield.

The kids got out of the van. Frankie, Jack and Regan were carrying spades. Tom was carrying a metal detector.

'I'm going to hide the van over there, behind those trees,' Darryl said. He pointed to a place a hundred metres away. 'If I see anyone coming, I'll sound the van's horn. Good luck!'

The kids climbed carefully over the gates. Tom put on

the headphones which were connected to the handle of the metal detector. Then the four friends started to search the ground carefully, metre by metre. They all looked carefully at the ground in front of them, and Tom moved the metal detector from side to side.

After he'd watched them climb over the gates, Darryl drove the van under the trees. He was very tired. He didn't like getting up at five o'clock in the morning. He tried to stay awake. But after a few minutes, he was asleep.

———

It was an hour later. The children had searched only a small area of the airfield.

'This is taking too long,' Reagan said angrily. 'We'll never find anything.' She looked up for a moment. Then she gasped. She pointed to the small hill over the old Ops Room.

'Look!' she whispered.

A line of women was walking over the grass. They were dressed in WAAF uniforms. A pale light was glowing all around them.

As the four friends watched them, the WAAFs disappeared into the hill, one by one.

Regan ran towards the women.

'Come back! Come back!' she shouted. But the women had gone.

Frankie, Jack and Tom followed Regan. Tom moved the metal detector over the grass on top of the little hill. Suddenly, there was a sharp sound in his headphones.

'There's a big piece of metal under here,' he said. 'Quickly! Dig, everybody!'

The kids started to dig with their spades. Ten minutes later, they had found a big black metal hatch – a door in the ground. The hatch was two metres long and one metre wide. It had two large metal handles.

The four friends pulled on the handles and slowly, the heavy hatch opened. Underneath it, they saw some concrete steps. And at the bottom of the steps there was a red metal door.

Regan ran down the steps first and Tom followed her. Together, they pulled on the handle of the red door. The door slowly opened. Inside, they saw a brightly lit corridor. Its walls were white and there were grey wooden doors along both sides of it. Electric lights hung from the ceiling. Everything looked clean and new.

'We're back in 1940 again,' Regan said. 'Come on. Glen has brought us here for a reason.'

Jack and Frankie came down the steps. They all went through the red door, and they closed it behind them.

Now the friends could hear sounds – the sounds of typewriters, the sounds of women's voices. Suddenly, one of the grey doors opened. A woman in WAAF uniform came out of it and walked towards the red door. She passed the children, but she didn't see them.

'She can't see us. She's a ghost!' Frankie said.

'No, *she's* not the ghost – *we* are the ghosts!' Jack replied. 'She's not in our time. We're in *hers*!'

The friends walked on down the corridor. Then they stopped and looked through an open doorway. They saw a room which was full of women who were sitting at desks. They were using typewriters. They were very busy. A calendar on the wall gave the date – 28TH AUGUST 1940.

———

Darryl was still asleep in his van. It was now seven o'clock. He didn't see the Facelift Construction trucks drive onto the airfield. He didn't hear the bulldozer's engine start. At ten past seven, big machines began to dig into the hill over the old Ops Room.

———

Darryl was sleeping in 1999, but below the hill the kids were still in 1940. And it was the day of the big German attack on Lychford Green – the 28th of August.

The four friends walked to the end of the corridor. On the left was a grey metal door.

'We must go through there,' Jack said. But suddenly, a bell began to ring loudly. The ground around them shook. Then the kids heard the thud of exploding bombs.

'German bombers are attacking the airfield!' Tom shouted.

'Come on,' Jack said, and he pushed open the metal door. A young woman in WAAF uniform was standing just inside it. Her back was towards the doorway.

Behind the woman, there was a big room. There was a table in the middle of it, covered with a huge map. More young women were moving small coloured flags across it. This was the Ops Room itself! Some men in RAF uniforms were sitting on a high platform at the back of the room. There were many phones on the long desk in front of them. One of the men was Squadron Leader Leighbridge-Smith.

The young WAAF turned towards the kids. Frankie remembered the photo which she had seen the day before.

'Florrie Skinner!' she said.

Florrie looked at the four friends and smiled.

'Don't be frightened,' she said. 'I won't hurt you.' Her fingers touched Jack's shoulder.

'She can see us! She can touch us!' Regan said quietly. 'The others can't see us, but Florrie can.'

The kids went back into the corridor. There was another metal door on the other side of it. Jack was going to open this door. But at that moment, there was a terrible noise and then a tremendous explosion. The building was falling on top of them. They heard several more bombs exploding nearby. Next came the screams – the terrible screams.

13

Gone for Ever!

The four friends were thrown against a wall. Their eyes and mouths were full of dust. Then Regan saw a light in front of them. A shape was standing there.

'It's Glen! He's going to help us!' Regan shouted. 'Come on! This way!'

The children followed the ghost back along the corridor. Now the corridor was old and dirty. They were not in 1940 any more. They were in the present. But Glen was still with them.

The phantom airman pointed to a door. The kids pushed the door open and walked into a small room. There was a desk in the room and a bookcase.

Glen pointed to the bookcase and moved his arm.

'There's something behind this bookcase,' Regan said. 'We must push it away from the wall.'

A moment later, they were looking at a small black metal door in the wall. It was the door to a small safe.

Regan pulled the handle. 'I can't open it,' she said. 'It's locked!' As she spoke, the light from the ghost faded. The room was dark.

'Now I understand Glen's message,' Jack said. 'He was telling us about the safe. He wanted us to find it. He was saying, "Help me rest. Safe under the airfield." Then he was going to tell us what was inside the safe.'

Suddenly, there was a sound in the corridor. The kids saw the light of a torch.

'We must hide! Get under the desk!' Jack whispered.

A fat man came into the room. He shone his torch onto the wall and quickly found the safe. He took a key from his pocket. A moment later, the door of the safe opened. Then the man bent down and they saw his face in the light of the torch. It was Terry Bowles! The businessman was laughing quietly.

'Where did you put them, Grandfather, you wicked old man?' he said to himself. 'Ah yes, here they are.'

He took a little black bag out of the safe and opened it. He shone the light from his torch into the bag.

Suddenly, a bright, glowing light shone behind him. Glen had come back!

Terry Bowles turned and saw the phantom airman. The fat man screamed. He was terrified. He dropped the little bag and he fell to the floor. He started to crawl towards the door of the room on his hands and knees. Glen moved towards him. Terry Bowles screamed again and jumped up. He reached the door, and he ran!

A moment later, Regan got out from under the desk. She walked towards Glen. He was covered with glowing light now, and he was smiling at her. All the burns and cuts had gone from his face. He was the handsome young pilot in Florrie's photo again.

Regan held out her hand to him and Glen touched it. Then he pointed to the floor and Regan looked down. There were small bright lights all over the floor. They were diamonds!

The girl looked up again, but now Glen's light was fading. A moment later the phantom airman had gone for ever!

14

The Kids

It was two weeks later. The four friends had given their project about Lychford Green airfield to Mrs Tinker. She had been very pleased with it.

'You've found out so much,' she had said. 'A lot of your facts surprised me. And they surprised Mr Ballard at the museum too. No one knew how the Ops Room was organized.'

Now the kids were sitting in Regan's garden. The American girl was reading an article in the *Lychford Gazette*.

'Listen to this,' she said. 'The newspaper says, "Terry Bowles, the owner of Facelift Construction, heard the children shouting. He went down into the Ops Room to save them." That isn't true!'

'He didn't come to save us. He wanted to get the diamonds,' Frankie said. 'But Glen stopped him!'

'The paper doesn't say anything about Glen,' Jack said. 'And we didn't either. We couldn't, could we?'

'No,' Tom replied. 'Mrs Tinker doesn't believe in ghosts. But we do – and Terry Bowles does too!'

'The next part is terrible,' Regan said. She read from the newspaper again. 'It says, "Terry Bowles saved the young people – he is a hero. But his grandfather wasn't a hero – he was a traitor! Mr Bowles found his grandfather's diary. Squadron Leader Alfred Leighbridge-Smith had been working for the Germans. He was a spy. And he was in charge of lots of other spies. The Germans had given him a bag of diamonds. He was going to pay his spies with them." Well that part is true! But listen to this! "Mr Bowles will not keep the diamonds. He is going to use them for Lychford. He is going to build a museum under the airfield. It will make Lychford famous! Mr Bowles is a hero!" That's what it says! The article is wrong! Terry Bowles is *not* a hero!' Regan shouted suddenly. She threw the newspaper onto the ground.

'Glen was the hero,' Jack said.

'Yes, and Glen is happy now. I'm glad about that,' Regan said. 'And we've told Florrie Skinner the truth about the crash. I'm glad about that too. Glen tried to save the evacuees. He died because he tried to save them. He wanted us to help him rest. And now, he *can* rest.'

'We'll always remember him,' Frankie said. 'And we'll always remember those poor children.'

Regan looked at her friends for half a minute. Then she took an envelope from her pocket.

'Florrie gave me this,' she said.

Regan took a small picture from the envelope – a photo of four children. There were a few words written on the back of it: *THE KIDS – AUGUST, 1940.*

The friends looked at the old picture of the four young evacuees. In the photo, they were standing close together. The two boys had fair hair. One of the girls was very pretty. She had fair hair. The other girl was younger and shorter. Her hair was long and dark.

'It's us!' Regan whispered. '*We* are those children! Florrie Skinner didn't see the ghosts of the evacuees in the underground room that day. She saw *us*!'

For a moment, everything was quiet. Then suddenly, a plane roared across the sky above them. It was a Spitfire!

Points for Understanding

1

The four friends see a Spitfire. What is a Spitfire?

2

The kids have been in the middle of a storm, but Darryl has not seen the storm. What has happened? Make a guess.

3

'Did the crash happen on the same date, many years ago?' asks Tom. 'Yes, that's exactly what I think,' Darryl replies. Why does he think this?

4

Frankie and Regan want to talk to Florrie Skinner. Why?

5

Regan says, 'I can't do anything. It's too late. It happened nearly sixty years ago.' Explain why she says this.

6

Florrie asks the girls to find her photo of Glen. Why does she ask them to do this?

7

Regan finds a piece of metal at the airfield. Has Glen helped her to find it? If he has, how has he done this?

8

After the piece of metal has scratched the word 'TRAITOR' on the table, Regan takes the metal to her bedroom, and then all the kids go into the kitchen. Why do they do these things?

9

'No, Glen, No!' Regan shouts. 'Don't hurt her.' What is Glen doing? Why is he doing it? Make a guess.

10

When the kids are in the old plane above Lychford Green, they are taken back into the past. What happens in 1999 while the kids are in the past? Give a reason for your answer.

11

When Jack touches the diary, it is very, very cold. What other things in the story are cold when one of the kids touches them? What do you learn from this?

12

'As the four friends watched them, the WAAFs disappeared into the hill ...' By the end of this chapter, the reader understands this strange sight. Explain what happened.

13

'Now I understand Glen's message,' Jack says. Why didn't the four friends understand it before?

14

At the end of the story, the friends look at the photo of the four evacuees and they understand something. They don't only look like the dead children, they are really the same people. How do the four friends know this?

Macmillan Heinemann English Language Teaching
Between Towns Road, Oxford OX4 3PP
A division of Macmillan Publishers Limited
Companies and representatives throughout the world

ISBN 0 333 79887 2

First published Macmillan Children's Books (1999)
This retold version for Heinemann ELT Guided Readers
Text © Macmillan Publishers Limited 2000
Design and illustration © Macmillan Publishers Limited 2000
Heinemann is a registered trademark of Reed Educational & Professional Publishing Limited
This version first published 2000

Designed by Sue Vaudin
Illustrated by Annabel Large
Cover by Jim Friedman and Marketplace Design
Typeset in 11.5/14.5pt Goudy
Printed and bound in Spain by Mateu Cromo SA

2004 2003 2002 2001 2000
10 9 8 7 6 5 4 3 2 1